Michael's Tree

By L.A. Eaton

Illustrated by Monica J. Wadsworth

WestBow Press books may be ordered through booksellers or by contacting:

WestBow Press
A Division of Thomas Nelson & Zondervan
1663 Liberty Drive
Bloomington, IN 47403
www.westbowpress.com
844-714-3454

Interior Image Credit: Monica J. Sager

ISBN: 978-1-6642-6599-8 (sc)
ISBN: 978-1-6642-6600-1 (e)

Library of Congress Control Number: 2022908347

Print information available on the last page.

WestBow Press rev. date: 08/30/2022

WESTBOW
PRESS®
A DIVISION OF THOMAS NELSON
& ZONDERVAN

For all those who have continually encouraged me to keep writing.

Michael stood clad in a thin jacket staring longingly at the Christmas tree's price tag while clutching the tarnished coins in his hand. He'd counted his savings twice before heading out and knew he did not have enough to purchase the Christmas tree. His family had not been able to afford a tree for the past two years. This year he had hoped to show his baby sisters the splendor of a simple tree. A tree always made the house seem festive, more like a celebration, and he missed it.

Taking one last glance at the tree, he turned and headed for home, the swirling snow not stinging nearly as bad as his tears. He had prayed this year would be different, that Ma wouldn't feel so bad about not being able to provide more for them. Now Michael knew how she felt, for he too felt disappointment.

He would have traveled the remaining two blocks home in misery if the sound of a snow shovel grating against a wooden porch hadn't broken through his thoughts.

Seeing Mr. Olsen struggling with the snowy build up on his porch, he felt driven to offer a hand.

"Mr. Olsen, let me help you," said Michael, noticing the sweat under his gray hair.

"Oh, thank you," replied Mr. Olsen with a smile. "I'm having quite a time with all that has fallen off the eaves."

"Do you think the snow will stay through Christmas?" asked Michael as he took the shovel and threw his skinny body against it to loosen the pile.

"I don't rightly know," Mr. Olsen replied and blew his drippy nose into a handkerchief.

They continued their idle chatter as Michael cleared the porch for safe travel. Placing the shovel near the door, Michael bid Mr. Olsen good day. To his surprise he hadn't made it one step down the porch when Mr. Olsen stopped him.

"You're a hard worker, Michael," he said placing a shiny coin in Michael's palm. "You have a Merry Christmas."

"Thank you, Mr. Olsen," gushed Michael as a twinkle formed in his eye. Quickly he calculated how much more would be needed for his tree. "Thank you, and Merry Christmas to you, too!"

The sweat he'd worked up was beginning to freeze under his worn flannel jacket, but the cold could not extinguish his renewed hope. Passing Old Lady Harding's on his way to his yard, he stopped and surveyed her porch. She had not been out, and the porch looked as though she couldn't get out even if she had wanted. The blowing snow had drifted in front of her door blocking any entrance or exit.

Never missing any of the neighborhood action, Old Lady Harding's face stared menacingly out of the corner window at Michael.

Michael waved cheerfully at her, surprising them both. He decided then and there not to let Old Lady Harding's grumpiness get to him. He marched up to her porch, grabbed the shovel propped in the corner, and began to dig her out of her house. She peered out at him occasionally, but Michael knew better than to expect even so much as a thank you from the bitter old lady. Nevertheless, while walking home, he jingled the coins in his pocket with satisfaction and a bright outlook for the next day.

Michael awoke before the sun and planned how to earn the last few coins. The snow had continued throughout the night, covering everything under a thick blanket. He headed out, snow shovel in hand, to the General Store and was rewarded with another coin. After a morning of shoveling, his pocket was heavy with coins, and he walked proudly to the Christmas tree lot.

"I'd like to purchase a tree, Sir," Michael said to the lot attendant looking around hopefully for the tree he had admired the day before.

"Not many left, son, but you are welcome to any we have."

Michael saw several much too large for him to afford but did not see the one he had hoped for.

"Sir, I was here yesterday, and you had one about this tall," Michael said holding his hand slightly above his head. "I'd like that one, please."

"Son, all we have are the larger ones."

"But I worked all morning to earn the rest of the money," choked Michael through a tightened throat, while tears threatened once again.

The attendant looked at the young boy's lean form, rosy cheeks, and tear-filled eyes. Softly he asked, "How much do you have, son?"

"Ten dollars" Michael replied.

Without looking, the attendant knew he didn't have a tree for that price, but that wasn't to say he didn't have something to offer.

"Come with me," he said to Michael, and he led him to a tree that had some of the branches broken in transportation. "I know it isn't much, but if you put it in the corner, the broken branches won't show too much."

Michael looked at the tree. It sure wasn't what he had imagined. And then the attendant added, "I'll sell it to you at half-price. That should leave you enough for some candles."

The worry left Michael's eyes and was replaced with a wide grin. "You have a deal, Sir!"

Shovel across his shoulder and candles in his pocket, he lugged the tree down the road toward home with content in his heart. Tomorrow his sisters would wake up to a true Christmas celebration.

Passing Old Lady Harding's, he saw her peering into the street, a vulture's eye on all who passed. Feeling so good at the day's event, he once again shoveled her porch free of snow and waved cheerfully at her as he left.

"Michael! Michael!" his sisters cried as he entered the house.

"I brought you a tree," he announced to them. "Now get out of the way so I can get it through the door!" he added laughing. He looked at his ma sheepishly as she stood in the kitchen with a hand on her hip and her lips in a tight line.

"Ma, I bought it for the girls with money I earned," he explained. "I thought they would like it."

"So, they will," said Ma smiling, "so they will."

It was a festive night, with the stringing of popcorn and the hanging of ornaments. Jessica, two, needed the most help and fell sleep in the corner among the tattered blankets. Ruth, Jessica's elder by two years, endured much longer, contributing many paper ornaments herself, before she too joined her sister in dreamland.

Ma sat quietly in the light of the fire tying ribbon into bows for the tree and looking at her eleven year-old who'd grown into quite a young man. As Michael helped her put the finishing touches on the scantly decorated tree, he said, "I'll be right back Ma. I have a surprise."

Returning with a dozen candles, Ma nodded her head in approval. Placing the candles strategically to fill in the empty spots, he couldn't stop thinking of Old Lady Harding.

"Ma, why is Old Lady Harding so miserable all of the time?"

"What makes you ask that?"

"Well," he thought momentarily, "we don't have much, and Christmas hasn't always been the greatest."

He stopped abruptly hoping he hadn't spoken harshly, that he hadn't hurt his ma's feelings. When she didn't respond he continued, "I mean, it hasn't made us ornery."

Ma smiled. "No, we have each other, and God watches over us. If we didn't have each other, life would be much harder. I think Mrs. Harding may be angry that she didn't have any children, that she's alone."

"Oh," Michael responded thinking all of this over. "I guess it would be lonely without a family."

"Yes, my son, it would," she said and kissed him good night.

Ruth's cries of delight woke both Michael and his sister.

"Michael, come and look!" she exclaimed jumping on him.

Laughing, he allowed her to drag him over to the tree where Ma had already lit the candles. They twinkled a cheery good morning to every one of the children. Jessica was in Ma's arms, her sleepiness wearing off, and Ruth looked on with big eyes drinking in the splendor of the tree. Michael looked past the misshapen poorly decorated tree. The joy and warmth it brought to the room made it the most marvelous tree his eyes had ever seen.

Ma had her children around her looking at the tree when a knock came at the door. To everyone's surprise Old Lady Harding stood on the opposite side.

"Morning, June," she spat at Ma. "Brought you and the young ones some breakfast."

Thrusting the fresh bread and apple butter into Ma's hands she turned to go, but not before Ruth could shout out in excitement.

"Come look at our tree!" Grabbing Old Lady Harding's hand Ruth pulled. "It's in here."

Ma quickly invited her in, and since Ruth wouldn't let her go, she had no choice.

Old Lady Harding looked at the pathetic tree and didn't know how to respond.

"Lights. Purdy lights," pointed out Jessica and stuck her thumb back in her mouth.

"Yes, it has lights, pretty lights," Old Lady Harding repeated, for even though the rest of the tree was cockeyed, it was true, the candles were pretty.

"Can we open our presents, Ma," asked Ruth. "Can we, please?"

"Not until we remember what this day is about," said Ma.

"I should be going," Old Lady Harding said as she headed for the door.

"Nonsense," replied Ma redirecting her to a chair, and it was settled. Then Ma began as Old Lady Harding fidgeted restlessly.

"A long time ago there was a poor family not unlike ourselves, and the mother was pregnant. But it was a special baby, one that God had given her."

"I really must go," interrupted Old Lady Harding feeling angry that God had not given her any children. "This is your family Christmas."

Ma just put her hand on Old Lady Harding's shoulder and said, "stay" before continuing. "It was a special baby because God was His daddy, and God gave Him to the whole world."

"I thought He gave the baby to Mary?" Ruth asked clearly confused now.

"He did Ruth, but only to take care of. God sent the baby for everyone."

There was a sniffle on the other side of the room, and Michael was surprised to see tears in Old Lady Harding's eyes.

"Are you okay?" he asked her.

She glared at Michael and turned to June spitting, "What do you mean He gave the baby to everyone? I never had any babies."

"God gave you His Son, Jesus," explained June softly. "Jesus was sent for you and for me. God gave Him up to Mary to raise as a human. Then God gave Him up as an adult to die for our sins. God loves you so much He gave up His only Son for you."

"Gave me His Son," Old Lady Harding whispered and began to sob. Ruth rushed over to comfort her as she had seen Ma do on numerous occasions.

Patting Old Lady Harding on the hand, Ruth said, "There, there."

Old Lady Harding chuckled through her tears as she pulled Ruth onto her lap and repeated, "God gave me His Son . . . go on, June."

"So, you see," continued Ma, "that Christmas isn't about trees or presents. It is about giving - God giving the greatest gift of all time to every man and woman, and when you accept that gift, Jesus lives within your heart forever."

"I was given a baby," smiled Old Lady Harding. Placing Ruth on the floor, she rushed out the door before anyone could stop her.

Ruth and Michael looked to Ma. Surely Ma knew why Old Lady Harding left so quickly. But Ma just looked at Michael with her mouth hanging open wondering herself what had gotten into Mrs. Harding.

Ma refocused the children's attention to their stockings, and the two girls forgot all about Old Lady Harding, but Ma and Michael were left burning with curiosity. The stockings each held an orange and a stick of candy. Jessica and Ruth's both had rag dolls. However, the food was all Michael's stocking held, and Ma looked to him with an apology in her sorrow filled eyes.

As the girls danced around the tree with their new dolls, a rapid knock came at the door before it opened abruptly, and Old Lady Harding came bustling in from the cold.

"I didn't miss the gift giving, did I?" she gushed.

"Not completely," answered Ma puzzled.

"Good, good!" replied Old Lady Harding. "Come here, Jessica. I have something for you."

With Ma pushing her from behind, Jessica approached Old Lady Harding.

"Here, Jessica, this is for your hair," and she brought forth a strip of lacy ribbon with green thread adorning it.

Upon seeing Jessica's gift, Ruth marched right up to Old Lady Harding ready to receive her gift.

"And for you, Ruth," announced Old Lady Harding, "something for your tree."

Old Lady Harding pulled forth a star made of gold that made Ma gasp and Ruth "ooh and ahh".

"Help me put it on," demanded Ruth, and Old Lady Harding lifted her in the air so Ruth could set it upon the treetop. They all stood around the tree admiring the beautiful star.

"And for you, Michael, a special gift. For if it hadn't been for you, I would have never received my gift. Tell me Michael, what made you shovel my porch?"

"I was so happy about buying the tree. I wanted to do something nice," he stammered.

"Then it is the tree we must thank, for if you hadn't shoveled my porch, I wouldn't have felt compelled to bring over breakfast this morning."

Talking the entire time, she had walked to the door and reached outside to where she had placed the gift beside the door frame.

Michael couldn't believe his eyes when she handed him a sled, and he looked to Ma for approval. Ma smiled and nodded. Michael thanked her as he ran his hand over the smooth seat and slick runners, hoping it wasn't all a dream.

"Mrs. Harding," he asked, for Old Lady Harding no longer seemed appropriate. "Are you sure, Mrs. Harding?"

"Yes, Michael. I am sure," she smiled.

"Mrs. Harding, what was your gift?" asked Michael, looking up into the face that somehow had changed in the past hour.

"It was your Ma's story. I found out God gave me a son a long time ago. I just never accepted him. Now I have such joy in my heart, and all because of you and your Christmas tree."

 LA Eaton was raised in rural Michigan where her mother instilled in her a love of reading. She is a teacher and a lover of creative activities, nature, and adventure. She currently lives on Kodiak Island, Alaska with her husband of 19 years and two children. A lifetime journal keeper, LA Eaton uses her journal entries as a starting point for her inspirational children's stories and other writings.

 Monica felt honored and challenged by the invitation to draw the 1940's era scenery, characters, and vision for Michael's tree. While she does not have any formal art training, she has been drawing and painting since she was 5 years old and always found it to be a favorite hobby of hers next to music. On her Etsy shop you'll find drawings and watercolor paintings of animals, landscapes and still lifes. Her inspiration comes from the Pacific Northwest and Alaska where she lived for the last 15 years. In 2021 she and her Coast Guard husband and Golden Retriever were relocated to Corpus Christi, Texas. There, Monica runs her own private practice, Seeking Light Counseling, and continues to participate in local and state-wide art festivals, as well as sells art on her Etsy shop, Ivy and Oat.

Printed in the United States
by Baker & Taylor Publisher Services